Scooby Bakes a Cake

by Frances Ann Ladd

Illustrated by Duendes del Sur

SCHOLASTIC INC.

New York   Toronto   London   Auckland   Sydney
Mexico City   New Delhi   Hong Kong   Buenos Aires

Shaggy was hungry.
"Like, wow!" he said.
"It is way past
snack time!"

"Hey Scooby, come here! Help me make a cake. We need to use flour, sugar, butter, and eggs."

"Can you look
in the fridge?
Do we have any eggs?
We need
five whole eggs."

"Is there any milk?
We need milk.
Here is a little butter.
We need a little more.
Jeepers, that is all!"

"Take the sugar
and put it in here."
Scooby put Scooby
Snacks in, too.
Then he put the cake
in the oven to bake.

When the cake was done,
Shaggy took it
out to cool.
"You taste it first, Scoob."
Scooby took a bite.
"Do you like the cake?"

"This time I will take
a bite."
"Zoinks!" he said.
"Is this a joke?
It tastes like
Scooby Snacks!
Scooby Snacks are not
for people!"
Shaggy took
one more bite.

"Well, maybe they are for some people. Like me!"